The Mukluk Ball

www.mnhspress.org

The Minnesota Historical Society Press is a member of the Association of University Presses.

Manufactured in China.

10 9 8 7 6 5 4 3 2 1

∞ The paper used in this publication meets the minimum requirements of the American National Standard for Information Sciences–Permanence for Printed Library Materials, ANSI Z39.48-1984.

International Standard Book Number

ISBN: 978-1-68134-116-3 (hardcover)

Library of Congress Cataloging-in-Publication Data available upon request.

The Mukluk Ball

Katharine Johnson

Illustrations by Alicia Schwab

MINNESOTA
HISTORICAL
SOCIETY PRESS

"The Mukluk Ball!" Karhu said to Zazaa the owl. "I'm going for sure. One way or another, this is my year."

First, he needed a pair of mukluks.

He looked longingly at the Mukluk Store display. Then he saw another poster.

It just so happened that Karhu was a good berry picker. He could sell blueberries at the festival—if he didn't eat too many. He spent all the next day picking.

On the day of the festival he scratched a bark sign.

Berry lovers flocked to his booth. Karhu had decided to sell hugs, too. The Shagawa Square Dancers bought both. Millie, the do-si-do champion, liked Karhu's hugs so much that she came back three times.

Karhu sold all his berries. He counted the money. Yes! He had enough.

Now it was time to learn to dance.

Outside the Vanilla Mouse Café,
Karhu tuned his radio to music.
He laced up his mukluks.

LIBRARY OF FIN

READ

BOOKS

His do-si-do
friend Millie
twirled him in
a polka.

Mary Ann
the librarian
showed him the
boogie-woogie.

Inga the folksinger
taught him the
chachacha.

Youngsters led him
in the bunny hop.

All autumn Karhu swayed, glided, and whirled with his new friends. He could even tango—if he remembered to tie his laces.

Karhu tore
November from the
calendar. He counted. Six more
weeks until the Mukluk Ball!
He stretched and yawned.

"How will I ever wake up in time to go dancing?" Already his eyelids felt like they'd drop shut and not open for another three months.

Then he heard "Who, who-who, whooo-hooo?" Zazaa was hooting high up in a tree. "It's sleepy me," Karhu yawned.

"Zazaa, I need your help. Please
who-who me awake on January 15
so I can go to the Mukluk Ball."

"Sounds like a hooooot. I can
dooooooo that for yoooooooou,"
said Zazaa.

Snug in his den,
Karhu fell fast asleep.

Six weeks drifted
by as the snows fell.

"Who, who-who, whoo-hoo!" Zazaa fluttered to Karhu's den. "Time to get up for the ball."

"Already?" Karhu yawned and stretched. He pulled on his mukluks.

"Yippee!" he called as he headed to town. "I'm finally going to the Mukluk Ball!"

He tried a few dance steps on the way — just to make sure he remembered.

The Finn Hall band
played a polka.
Millie led him onto
the dance floor.
Mary Ann tangoed
and jitterbugged
with him.

"Conga time!" Everyone lined up behind Karhu. They all shimmied and shook.

"One-two-three hop. One-two-three spin. Toe tap right. Toe tap left." The conga line wiggled and waggled, pranced and danced. Around and around they went.

Karhu and Millie made up a dance called the Bear Hug Twist. All night he twirled and whirled, twizzled and spun. He'd never had so much fun.

At midnight, the band softly played the last waltz. Inga asked Karhu to dance. Soon he was sound asleep on her shoulder.

As the band packed up their accordions,
the Shagawa Square Dancers carried
Karhu to their bus.

At the Echo
Trail they pulled
him on a dogsled. Zazaa
whoo-whoo-ed and flew from
tree to tree, leading the way.

Back home, Karhu snored and dreamed
of dancing. His toes tapped in time to
the music of the Mukluk Ball.